Fortune Cookie Castle

Fortune Cookie Castle

BY LEE GRIMES

ILLUSTRATED BY
ANNETTE LeBLANC

DUTTON CHILDREN'S BOOKS · NEW YORK

Library of Congress Cataloging-in-Publication Data

Grimes, Lee.
  Fortune cookie castle/by Lee Grimes; illustrated by
Annette LeBlanc.
      p.   cm.
  Summary: Cap and Lisa encounter a monster, a ghost, and secret
passageways when they try to help Duke Lothrio free his castle
from an evil spell.
  ISBN 0-525-44588-9
  [1. Castles—Fiction.   2. Magic—Fiction.]   I. LeBlanc,
Annette, ill.   II. Title.   89-49166
PZ7.G88428Fo   1990   CIP
[Fic]—dc20   AC

Published in the United States by Dutton Children's Books,
a division of Penguin Books USA Inc.

Designer: Susan Phillips

Printed in U.S.A.   First Edition
10 9 8 7 6 5 4 3 2 1

for David Lee Grimes
L. G.

for Bob
A. L.

Contents

1

The Castle
That Vanished

 Cap and Lisa were racing around trees in the forest, playing Knights and Dragons, when they heard a strange sound. It was high and faint and scratchy, like a voice from a worn old record. Cap thought he could make out the words: "Come to the castle. Come to the castle."

"Did you hear that?" he asked his sister.

"I heard something," Lisa said. "Sort of a tinny sound, not much louder than a whisper."

"I thought it said, 'Come to the castle.'" As Cap looked around to see who might have spoken, he heard another noise, this one round and deep and satisfied.

"UURRP!"

"Who burped?" Cap shouted.

Lisa laughed. "It's funny, but it's creepy. Is somcone spying on us?" Nobody answered. Finally she said, "Let's go on with our game."

Cap and Lisa were on vacation with their parents in Europe. They had been dragged through museums and cathedrals and castles until they felt that they might as well have been on a school field trip. Actually, the castles hadn't been so bad. Cap and Lisa had enjoyed imagining what life was like when knights fought in tournaments and nobody had cars or telephones or refrigerators or television sets.

Their parents had decided to rest for a week in the hilly province of Beringia. Cap, who was captain of his soccer team at school, had his soccer ball with him for practice, and Lisa had her net to catch butterflies. But they wanted something else to do. There hadn't been room in their luggage for books and comics and tapes, so they made up a game—Knights and Dragons. Cap had named himself Sir Whambo the Mighty, and Lisa had decided to be Ironskin the Fire-Breather.

Now he was chasing her around pine trees, shouting threats. Though Lisa was a year younger than Cap, she was fast, and she laughed as she dodged him like a jackrabbit. Finally he cornered her against a fallen tree and slashed at her with an imaginary sword. "I'm slicing you into dragon salami!"

"You broke your sword on my scales," Lisa taunted him. "Whoosh! I'm breathing flames. I'm frying you to a crisp!"

"Your flames couldn't toast a muffin," he scoffed, slashing at her once more.

As Lisa picked up a pinecone to throw, the voice came again, stopping her. "Come to the castle. Come to the castle."

"I heard it clearly that time," said Lisa. "It's squeaky."

"Yeah, and it sounded closer," said Cap.

"UURRP!" The burp seemed to come from somewhere in the trees.

With more confidence than he felt, Cap called, "Come on out, whoever you are!"

Nobody appeared. Cap and Lisa peered between the trees and up into their branches but saw no one. They could hear the rustle of small animals and the hum and buzz of insects—but no noises that a person might make.

"Whoever it is is hiding," Lisa said. "And why is he saying 'Come to the castle'? The egg man told us there weren't any castles around here."

"He said there used to be one, but then it disappeared," Cap reminded her. He imitated the accent of the old farmer who brought eggs to the cottage their parents had rented. "Zees days, no castle, but zere ees a story, very old, zat a castle rested eetself not much far from here, long time ago. Hundreds of years, no?"

"Yes," Lisa said with a laugh. She carried on the imitation. "Eet belong of a duke who had ze crazy idea to teach hees peasants to read. For what good? one asks. One day ze peasants are come to ze castle for zeir lessons, but zey cannot see eet. Eet ees deesappear."

"Like zees!" Cap blew an imaginary puff of smoke from a pipe. "I still don't see how a castle could disappear. Castles just crumble into ruined walls and towers, all covered with moldy lichens. We've seen plenty of them this summer."

Lisa pretended that she had a pipe too and waved it in the air. "Ah, but ze story say ze castle ees enchanted. My greatgrandfazer say two children go search for eet and never come back. People search in ze forest and find nozzing, not a thread of clozing, and no castle also."

4

"And then he warned us that if we did find a castle, not to go inside," Cap said.

"But it wouldn't hurt us to look for it." Lisa picked up her butterfly net. "It doesn't matter if we don't find it. I can catch some butterflies."

"The voice came from that direction, away from the cottage," said Cap, pointing. "Let's go that way and try to find a high place and look around."

Sometimes the ground sloped downward to chestnut trees with spiny green burrs, and sometimes it rose among birches and tall pines. In the clearings, Cap and Lisa saw butterflies zigzag around small blue and white flowers. Once a deer broke from cover ahead of them and dashed into hiding again. They saw mushrooms on the ground and squirrels scrambling up tree trunks.

"If we're trying to get lost, we're succeeding," Lisa said. "We must have come at least a mile."

"I'd better mark a trail." Cap fished his Swiss army knife out of his pocket and carved a notch in the bark of a tree.

Clouds began to collect in the sky, darkening the forest until the trees rose like threaten-

ing shadows. The hum of insects and the rustling of small animals faded into silence.

"It's spooky in here," Lisa said. "Something could be waiting for us. Maybe we should go back."

They stopped so Cap could notch another tree. As he slipped his knife into his pocket, he felt a touch on his back, as light as a puff of wind. It nudged him forward.

"Did you push me?" he asked Lisa.

"No. I thought you pushed me."

Although the gentle nudge hadn't made him stumble, Cap didn't like to be pushed. "Who did that?" he snapped. "Stop it!"

As if in reply, the children heard, "Come to the castle. Come to the castle." The voice was still high and scratchy, but stronger than before. Then, loud and long, "UUURRRP!"

"UURRP yourself," Lisa said angrily, looking disgusted. "I want to know what's going on here. Let's go a little farther and see what we find. We can be careful."

They walked upward through more pine trees, alert for anything that might be strange or dangerous. Once a woodpecker startled them with its loud *rat-tat-tat.* Now and then, Cap cut a notch for their trail. When the clouds broke and the sun came out again, they felt less nervous. Finally they pushed bushes aside and found themselves high on a ridge, overlooking a valley.

Across the valley, on top of a hill, was a castle.

2

Duke Lothrio
and Bounce

 With its massive gray walls, the castle looked forbidding. Along the top stood battlements, blocks of stone alternating with open spaces for archers. Two towers could be seen rising behind the walls, and narrow windows high in the towers seemed to spy down on Cap and Lisa. A drawbridge had been raised in front of an iron gate.

"If there's a drawbridge, there must be a moat," Cap said. "We're just not high enough to see it from here."

Something round and brown on the underside of the drawbridge glittered in the sunlight.

Lisa pointed at it. "That looks like an eye

staring at us. If the castle is enchanted, maybe it has a magic eye to see who's coming. Or an evil eye to scare us away."

"Then why did the voice say, 'Come to the castle'?" Cap asked. "I don't get it. It's easy to see the castle. It's right there, plain as day. How could no one else have found it?"

"How should I know?" Lisa laughed and then shivered. "It's scary, but it's exciting. Let's go closer."

"Remember the egg man's warning."

Lisa glanced at her brother slyly. "We can go closer without going inside."

They walked down into the narrow valley, picking their way past trees and bushes. Traces of what could have been an old road, now overgrown with weeds, led them up to the top of the hill. The castle stood fifty yards away. A moat filled with water did encircle it. Going to the edge of the moat, Cap picked up a rock and threw it at the castle's stone walls. The rock hit with a *chunk!* and splashed into the water.

"Well, it's real," he said. "It's not some kind of mirage."

"But no one seems to be around. No tourists, nobody at all."

Cap studied the moat. Water filled a wide, deep ditch, reaching to a bank on one side, where he and Lisa were standing, and lapping at the castle walls on the other. "We couldn't get inside if we wanted to," he said.

As if in answer, the drawbridge dropped slowly forward on its iron chains. Then the gate at the castle entrance swung open mysteriously.

"If that was an invitation, where is everybody?" Cap asked.

"Let's just cross the drawbridge and peek through the gateway. That wouldn't be going inside," Lisa reasoned.

They tiptoed across planks rough with splinters. Cap tripped where some wood had rotted away, but he caught himself before falling.

When they reached the open gate, they could look across a dirt courtyard to the inner castle building. Three stories tall, with few windows, it was constructed of stone. A central section connected two wings. Two towers, one on each wing, rose twice as high as the building itself. A tall double doorway stood open.

"Well, I guess we've seen all we can see," Cap said.

Just at that moment, he and Lisa heard a

booming "UURRP!" At the same time, a sudden strong gust of wind blew them through the gateway. They staggered, almost falling to their knees.

"I won't be shoved around by a big burp!" Lisa exclaimed angrily. "Let's go back."

"I don't like it either, but since we're already inside, we might as well see what else there is," Cap said.

He took Lisa's hand as they crossed the courtyard and stepped through the tall double doorway. After passing a guardroom with swords and armor on the walls, they entered a long room with a high ceiling—a grand reception hall.

In the dim light that filtered through narrow windows, Cap and Lisa could make out banners hanging from the ceiling beams and shields and tapestries on the walls. The shields were decorated with broad stripes of different colors or with the painted heads of horses, lions, and bears. The tapestries were woven to show hunting scenes and battles and strangely dressed men and women. Near the walls, chairs and cushions rested on the stone floor, which was covered with rushes.

And, finally, there were people. At least

they looked like people. The only thing was, they were silent and still.

Women in long dresses and men in knee breeches stood here and there without shifting their feet or moving their hands or nodding their heads. Others sat on the furniture as stiffly as dummies in a store window. Two children pitched forward without falling, as if they had been frozen in place while running. At the far end of the room, in front of a large fireplace without a fire, a man sat in a high-backed chair and studied a game of chess.

"I don't like the looks of this," Lisa whispered. "Let's get out of here."

The man in the high-backed chair surprised them by moving a piece on his chessboard and looking up. He had a thin face, a long nose, and shoulder-length dark hair.

"Well!" he exclaimed cheerfully. "Welcome, welcome! I see you found us. Got a little help, I dare say. I hope you don't turn into toads. Tell me your names."

"Cap," said Cap.

"Lisa," said Lisa. "Excuse me, but did you say something about us turning into toads?"

"That's Sprod's idea. He's the wizard who works for me, although he acts like it's the

other way around, and I work for him. I am Duke Lothrio of Beringia. You've heard of me, of course."

"Not by name, I'm afraid," Lisa answered, "but there are a lot of people and places I don't know about." She saw that the duke wore a plum-colored jacket with a fur collar and had short green pants tied at the knees with bows. Below long stockings, he wore short boots.

The duke shook a finger at her. "The world is both smaller and larger than people think. That's one of my wise sayings, which I just thought of. Excuse me while I write it down." He picked up a sheet of parchment and scribbled on it with a quill pen. "I'm writing a book, *The Wisdom of Lothrio,* for my people to read. Especially my peasants, because they work so hard that they forget how wise I am. Except that I have temporarily run out of peasants. After Sprod enchanted the castle, not one of them could find it."

Cap was feeling confused. "If your peasants couldn't find the castle, how come we could see it?" he asked.

"Say *why,* not *how come,*" replied the duke, shaking his finger at Cap. "You'll have to ask

Sprod for the details. Enchantments are his department. Where are you from?"

"America," Lisa answered.

"You haven't heard of me, and I haven't heard of America," the duke said. "That's fair. I see that America is a place where you wear funny pants." Suddenly he shouted, "Bounce! Come here! We have guests."

A small boy dressed all in green came running in from a room off the grand hall. He leaped into the air and somersaulted, landing on his hands in front of the duke's table. Then he tried to flip back onto his feet but sprawled on the floor instead.

Duke Lothrio laughed. "Meet Bounce, my apprentice juggler and acrobat. Bounce, juggle some balls for our visitors."

Bounce jumped up quickly, unhurt. Taking three balls out of a pocket, he juggled two of them in the air. But when he tried adding the third, his timing failed. All three balls fell to the floor and bounced away like frogs hopping.

The duke laughed again and said, "Keep at it, Bounce. I hope I live long enough to see you get it right. Meet Cap and Lisa."

"Hello," Bounce said softly. He blushed and looked at the floor. "Sorry I'm so clumsy.

I do practice a lot." He shrugged his shoulders.

"I'm sure you'll soon juggle perfectly," Lisa assured him. Bounce gave her a big smile.

Cap waved at the motionless figures in the room. "What happened to everybody?"

"Ah, you noticed, did you?" replied the duke. "They were no good at hunting for his crystal ball, so Sprod turned them into statues until things get back to normal around here. That way we don't have to feed them, which would be a problem since the peasants are temporarily unable to trundle their carts of food to the castle because they can't see it. The only thing growing in the garden is broccoli. By the way, I suppose you have fresh eyes."

"I guess we do," replied Cap, who was becoming more confused with every word the duke spoke.

"Oh, I'm sure you do. Sprod's spell won't let people see the castle unless they have a chance of finding his crystal ball, and fresh eyes are needed for that. Anyone who finds it wins a reward, stuff with jewels on it, that sort of thing. Those who fail are turned into toads. Sprod likes to have toads around to catch the flies that get into his room. Personally, I wish you luck."

"You're making my head spin," Lisa exclaimed. "Why should anybody be turned into a toad for not finding something? That doesn't sound fair! Please tell us what you're talking about."

"Gladly, my dear girl," said the duke. "Drag up some chairs and sit down."

3

The Duke's Tale

 "Once I was the happiest of dukes. I had broad lands and brave knights and lots of peasants to till the fields and sing and dance at festivals. They sang off-key and got mixed up changing partners, but everyone had a jolly time. My knights had fun bashing each other in tournaments and hunting in my forests. The cook knew how to make eighteen kinds of pie. And every month we had a fair. Merchants and tradesmen came from all over to sell their goods. Jugglers, acrobats, and puppeteers entertained us."

Lisa raised her hand as if she were back in school.

"Yes?" The duke nodded at her.

"Was the cook turned stiff too?" she asked.

"No. Someone has to cook the broccoli. Even Sprod knows that. The cook's tried fried broccoli and baked broccoli and steamed broccoli, but it all tastes like broccoli. Did you ever eat broccoli pie? I don't recommend it.

"Only one tragedy marred my happiness," the duke continued. "My wife died giving birth. Our daughter was a pretty little wiggly thing, which surprised me because in my opinion most babies don't look like much. I named her Thistle. Since she was a duke's daughter, everyone called her Lady Thistle, even before she could walk. She learned to sing and weave and dance, to tell good poetry from bad, to whistle birdcalls, and to ride sidesaddle, which are all harder to do than you might think, especially riding sidesaddle. But I stray from my subject, which is Thistle. She grew prettier with each passing day. By the time she was thirteen, the knights were writing love sonnets to her."

"What's a sonnet?" Cap asked.

"It's a poem fourteen lines long. In an Italian sonnet, which is the kind Thistle liked, the first, fourth, fifth, and eighth lines have to end in words that rhyme, like *bright, right, might,* and *knight.* The second, third, sixth, and seventh lines have to end in words that rhyme too, like *hop, top, flop,* and *glop.* There are different ways to rhyme lines nine to fourteen. Most people mess it up.''

Duke Lothrio's eyebrows rose as if he were surprised at his own explanation. ''It's harder to write something short than to throw words all over the place,'' he said. ''Even so, you wouldn't believe how much mush the knights squeezed into their sonnets!

''Now, where was I? Oh, yes! When Thistle became sixteen, I had to start thinking about a suitable husband for her.''

''When she was so young?'' Lisa couldn't help asking.

The duke ignored her. ''About this time my court wizard died, and I had to hire a new one. I sent heralds around to sound their trumpets and shout news of the job opening. Several wizards submitted applications. Sprod had the best references—dukes and even a king— although now that I think about it, he may have threatened to turn them into toads if they didn't write good things about him.

''Sprod had traveled to far Cathay to study under the wise men of the Orient, and he had learned how to make magic fortune cookies. He bakes each one with a slip of paper inside, and when you break the cookie open, the paper contains a message. If you figure out what the message means, you can't go wrong. At least that's what Sprod claims.

"In Cathay, Sprod also bought a treasure, a world-class crystal ball. If you look into it and ask it where to find something or what is going on somewhere or what the future will be, a picture appears in the crystal ball to show you. If a place is really hard to find, the crystal ball may even show you a map. I lost my favorite hunting knife one day, and the crystal ball showed me the forest trails to follow and the creeks to cross and exactly where to look for it in a pile of leaves. They were oak leaves, if you want to make a note."

Neither Cap nor Lisa wanted to make a note. The duke shrugged.

"I began to notice that two knights especially, Sir Baggish and Sir Grung, were hanging around Thistle all the time. Baggish was big, and I liked him because he was good at bashing enemies. No robber bands dared raid my dukedom while Baggish was around. He was honest and loyal too. He dedicated his tournament victories to Thistle, and he wrote her sonnets. Awful stuff! They made Thistle laugh, they were so bad.

"Anyway, she liked Baggish because he was strong and handsome and devoted to her. He wasn't very bright, but he was kindhearted and thoughtful. He warned enemies to run away before he bashed them. He offered his arm to old people who needed help. He gathered sunflower seeds for Thistle to feed to the birds."

"He helped me too," Bounce put in. "He held his hand under my back so I wouldn't fall when I was learning to do flips. It took weeks."

"Thistle wanted to marry Sir Baggish," the duke went on, "and that was all right with me, even if he was dumb. She had brains enough for both of them. She kept the castle records, and she always gave me an exciting chess match.

"Sir Grung wanted to marry Thistle, even though he knew she preferred Baggish. He and Baggish got along until they became rivals over Thistle. Grung was pretty good at bashing, and he was smart. He could add numbers without counting on his fingers. Once he almost beat me at chess. He wrote good sonnets with clever rhymes for Thistle. Love can't live on sonnets alone, however. That's one of my wise sayings."

"How come Thistle didn't like Grung best?" Lisa asked.

"I'm sure you meant to ask *why,* not *how come,*" the duke said, waggling his finger again. "Anyway, Grung was mean. He played sneaky tricks that nobody else thought were funny. Once in a tournament he bribed a squire to loosen the saddle straps on the horse of another knight, and the knight fell off as soon as the horse started to gallop. He liked to drip grease on a stairway so people would skid and tumble down the last few steps. He would stand there laughing as they fell. Another time, he went around at night cementing everybody's shoes to the floor. The best I can say for Grung is that he was as clean as fresh linen. Every day he went for a swim in the moat.

"Grung decided that the only way he could get Thistle to marry him was with the help of Sprod, the wizard. Sprod's rooms are on the top floor of the north tower. He has a laboratory where he mixes magic spells and a reception room where he keeps a tank for his toads. The toads were probably hopping around the room catching flies when Grung knocked. Sprod keeps the shutters open to let plenty of flies in. It seems to me that if he were to close them, he wouldn't need the toads, but I guess Sprod is fond of toads. Myself, I think dogs and cats have more personality.

"Most people who visit Sprod want a peek into his crystal ball, so he displays it in a case with his other treasures, like a golden spell sprinkler and a matched pair of petrified bats.

"But Grung didn't care about the crystal ball. He wanted Sprod to make him a love potion so that Lady Thistle would fall in love with him and marry him.

"Sprod has never gone in for love potions. He says tampering with emotions always causes trouble. So Grung asked for a fortune cookie instead, one that would tell him how to win Thistle's heart.

"Sprod went into his laboratory, where he bakes the fortune cookies and casts his magic spells. He keeps the cookies in a big brown jar.

"While Sprod was out of the room, Grung stole the crystal ball. Apparently he had come prepared to steal it, to get a hold over Sprod. Grung slipped it into a cloth sack attached to

his belt and replaced it with a ball of glass that he had been given by a lady of the court who collects junk you wouldn't believe."

Cap interrupted. "How do you know all this?"

"Sprod figured it out and told me later. When he came out of his laboratory, he gave Grung a fortune cookie. The fortune read: *You can't make cake from burnt toast.*

"Grung explained that his spell writes the fortunes, and that a lot of the time he doesn't have any idea what they mean. But he thought this one was saying you can't make a good marriage from a bad match.

"Grung muttered at that, but he said thank you before he left. Everyone, even Grung, knows you have to be polite to Sprod. Sprod gets angry at people who don't treat him with respect. When he's really mad, he turns them into things like teapots or rusty nails and won't turn them back until he thinks they've learned their lesson. Grung was too smart to be turned into a rusty nail before he had Sprod where he wanted him."

4

Sprod

 The duke shook his head sadly at the thought of what Grung had done. "The next day we were all having some really great fried oat porridge for lunch and admiring Thistle's new green dress when Sprod came running down the stairs bellowing curses.

"'Great howling grasshoppers!' he cried, charging into the hall. 'Mountains of mud! Where's my crystal ball?' He was carrying his golden spell sprinkler and the glass ball that Grung had left behind. Raising the ball high, he said, 'I asked this thing where I could find more petrified bats, and it was blank! It's a fake!' He threw it to the floor, smashing it to splinters. 'Somebody stole my crystal ball!'

"Grung spoke right up. 'I stole it.' He stood calmly with his arms folded. 'I hid it. I won't give it back until you give me the love potion I want.'

" 'Tell me where it is right now or I'll turn you into a dirty carpet and hang you on a line where everyone can beat the dust out of you,' Sprod threatened, waving his spell sprinkler.

" 'Then I won't be able to tell you where the crystal ball is, will I?' Grung replied with a sly grin. 'You'll have to find it on your own.'

" 'How can I find my crystal ball without my crystal ball?' Sprod wailed.

" 'Just give me the potion to make Lady Thistle want to marry me, and I'll tell you where it is.'

" 'I'd rather marry a petrified bat than you, Grung!' Thistle stormed. 'I don't want a sneak thief for a husband. I want a man who's honest and who respects my feelings.' She put her hand on Sir Baggish's arm and said, 'Baggish, make Grung tell where he hid the crystal ball.'

"Sir Baggish knew only one way to make anyone do anything. Bash him. But first he said courteously: 'Yield, Sir Grung, or I will have to challenge you to combat. If I win, you must tell us where the crystal ball is. If you win, I will leave Beringia, and you can try your luck with Thistle.'

"Everybody grinned at that, and Thistle laughed, because nobody thought Grung had a chance against Baggish."

"Then why didn't Grung yield?" Cap asked.

"Because he was too angry at not getting what he wanted. Besides, Grung had to accept the challenge or be judged a coward, and the peasants would throw rotten carrots at him. So Grung and Baggish put on their armor and helmets and flailed at each other with their swords. Usually the only entertainment we have at lunchtime is some knight plucking the strings of a lute and singing fancy nonsense about his adventures. Baggish and Grung put on a good show, clanging their swords, circling and swinging, leaping in and dodging back.

"Unfortunately, Baggish forgot that he was only supposed to batter Grung to the floor and demand that he yield or swallow cold steel. Baggish got carried away. He smashed the shield out of Grung's hand and swung a mighty blow that sliced straight through Grung's neck. Grung's helmeted head clattered to the floor, and blood flowed all over the place.

"Lady Thistle was aghast. She thought Baggish had overdone it. Baggish apologized to her for forgetting his own strength. Then he bent down and said into Grung's ear, 'Friend Grung, please forgive me. It was an accident.' Turning to Sprod, he asked, 'You can bring him back to life, can't you?'

" 'Of course not, you fool!' Sprod roared. 'I work magic, not miracles. How can he tell us where the crystal ball is now? I'll teach you to be so dumb! I'll turn you into a monster to guard the dungeon. That's all you're good for!'

"Before anyone could say a word, Sprod had sprinkled some drops of enchantment on Baggish. Poor Baggish turned into a monster right before our eyes. He looked something like a lizard because he was scaly and had a tail; something like a beetle because he was low and broad; something like himself because he was as long as he had been tall; something like a crocodile because his jaws had daggerlike teeth sticking out all over; and something like a bear because all four feet had sharp claws. And he smelled something like moldy goat cheese. Phew!

"The Baggish monster stood there, looking confused. Of course, it had never been a monster before, and I guess it takes some getting used to. Sprod tied a rope around its neck and dragged it away.

"I was sorry to lose a good basher like Baggish, but I felt cheerful at gaining a monster to guard the dungeon. Lady Thistle took a different view.

" 'I can't marry a monster!' she fumed. 'When Sprod gets angry, he's like a pot boiling over. He rushes into whatever he wants without thinking about anyone else. He'd set fire to the castle just to warm his toes on a cold night. I want Baggish, not a squat, ugly monster with butcher knives for teeth. I'm going to hide in my secret room and weave tapestries and sing to my birds until Sprod sends Baggish back to me.'

"Thistle ran out of the hall, but I wasn't worried. Secret, shmecret. Her room is on the second floor near the south tower. I thought I'd let her rage awhile and then go comfort her. That's how much I knew.

"Sprod came back chuckling and announced that he had tied the monster to an iron ring at the top of the dungeon steps. 'Don't worry about Baggish,' he said. 'He'll change back from a monster into the big lunkhead that he always was when a girl kisses him.'

"But none of the ladies of my court was willing to kiss a scaly, foul-smelling creature that might bite their heads off. Let Thistle do it, they said. She's the one who wants to marry Baggish. So I sent three ladies to Thistle's room to fetch her.

"Thistle wasn't there. She did have a secret room, after all. And since nobody could find her, they couldn't tell her how she could rescue Baggish from monsterhood."

5

More Spells

 After a pause, while Cap and Lisa thought of how Thistle had trapped herself, Duke Lothrio continued his story.

"Meanwhile Sprod warned us that if someone didn't find his crystal ball in three days, he would take drastic measures.

" 'Why don't you just bring the crystal ball back, using your golden spell sprinkler?' I asked him.

" 'Because spells don't work on something that's already enchanted, and the crystal ball works because it's enchanted.'

"Since the crystal ball was about the size of two fists, I didn't think it would be hard to find. What made it tricky was that it was transparent: You could see through it to whatever was behind it. I led search parties into the towers, despite a certain creakiness in my joints. We looked in closets and in corners, on top of beams and behind tapestries, in the oven and in the flour bin, under mattresses, inside empty suits of armor—everywhere. We searched high and low and sideways. But we couldn't find Sprod's crystal ball.

"In three days Sprod came down to the reception hall carrying his golden spell sprinkler and his brown jar of fortune cookies.

" 'Haven't found it, have you?' he said grimly. 'I baked a few fortune cookies to see what help they might give.'

"While everyone watched, I took a cookie and read the message out loud. The fortune was: *Stale problems need fresh eyes.* I thought it probably meant that we needed some new people to come looking for the crystal ball. I wasn't crazy about the idea of having peasants and strangers poke around my castle and track mud through it, however.

" 'Hmmm,' Sprod hmmmed thoughtfully. 'Seems to me the freshest eyes are children's eyes,' he finally said.

"I ate the first fortune cookie—which was nice and crisp, quite tasty, really—and broke open another. Its message was: *It takes born talent to see what can't be seen.*

"That made no sense to me, so I took a third cookie. Its message was: *Someone who finds a hidden place can find a hiding place.* 'That's silly,' I said. 'A hidden place *is* a hiding place.'

" 'No it isn't.' Sprod liked to contradict me without my permission. He hmmmed and thought for a while. 'Did Grung leave the castle after he stole my crystal ball?' he asked.

" 'No, sir,' answered one of the castle guards. 'He took his swim but he never left the castle grounds.'

" 'Then the hiding place must be in the castle,' Sprod reasoned. 'But the castle is not hidden. Anyone can see it.'

"I looked for more fortunes in the jar, but all I found was cookie dough. Sprod reached into the jar and ate the dough absentmindedly, going 'Hmmm' thoughtfully between bites.

" 'I've got it!' he exclaimed at last, and burped. 'The beauty of magic is that it's logical. All you have to do is think upside down and backward. To find my crystal ball, someone must find a hidden place that holds the hiding place. The hiding place is in the castle, but the castle isn't hidden. Therefore, I have to hide it, which I'll do by making it invisible. Then the castle won't be seen except by the few people who are born with the talent to see it.

" 'It's a big job, making a castle disappear. Your run-of-the-mill wizard couldn't do it.' He took a deep breath and burped. 'UURRP!'

"Before I could object that invisibility might be a bit of a bother, and that it would be simpler if he just got a new, improved crystal ball, Sprod raised his spell sprinkler. Lightning flashed from its tip, and sparks flew through the room and out the windows. I waited, but nothing else seemed to happen.

" 'We didn't disappear,' I said, with a feeling of relief.

" 'Ah, but the castle did,' Sprod answered. 'I raised a cloak of invisibility around the moat. Anyone on our side can see what's beyond it. But people outside the cloak won't be able to see the castle unless they have the born talent. Young people with fresh eyes and the talent will come along someday.'

" 'Someday?' I asked. 'How long will it take?'

" 'Who knows?' Sprod answered. 'Maybe a day or two, maybe a thousand years. Don't worry. Nobody grows older in an enchanted castle.' He squinted at everyone assembled in my grand hall. 'There won't be anything for

you people to do while we wait. UURRP! I'll fix it so you won't know any time has passed at all.' He raised his spell sprinkler. 'Relax. This won't hurt.'

"Suddenly all the knights and ladies and commoners in the hall, even the children, turned as stiff as broccoli stalks, the way they are now. Everyone except me and Bounce and the cook and the monster who had been Sir Baggish."

"Why wasn't Bounce enchanted?" Cap asked.

"Because I was dressed all in green, from my cap to my boots," Bounce answered. "Enchantments don't work if you're covered in green."

"Sprod left the cook out because he needed him," the duke said. "And it would be rude and uppity, most improper, to enchant a noble employer. Baggish couldn't be enchanted again because he already was."

"What about Lady Thistle?" Lisa asked.

"I suppose she was wearing her new green dress. She's probably in her secret room right now, wasting time when she could be down here losing to me at chess.

"'Very impressive, old boy,' I said to Sprod as my eye roved over what looked like a hall of statues, 'but people—children especially—don't wander around hunting for invisible castles.'

" 'I'm not finished,' Sprod said. He told Bounce to run up to his reception room and get one of his petrified bats."

"It was like an ugly piece of brown stone," said Bounce.

"Sprod began whispering to the bat, which started to move its wings. I couldn't make it all out, but he seemed to be ordering the bat to fly throughout Beringia looking for children who had the born talent to see what can't be seen. I think the bat was supposed to tell them to come to the castle. It was hard to hear because Sprod kept burping from all the cookie dough he had eaten. Then he touched the petrified bat with the spell sprinkler, and it vanished.

"After a year or so, a couple of kids wandered across the drawbridge, and I set them to searching for the crystal ball. Sprod gave them fortune cookies to help, but they couldn't figure out the fortunes. After a few hours Sprod grew impatient and turned them into toads. It was a long time before any more young people found the castle, and they wound up as toads too. Others have come and joined the search. Alas! Toads every time."

6

Dealing with
a Wizard

 Cap and Lisa looked at each other uneasily when Duke Lothrio had finished.

"That was a very sad story," Cap said, "and it's too bad we can't make it have a happy ending." He thought their own story might have a sad ending if they didn't leave quickly, so he said, "We don't have fresh eyes. We've been using ours all our lives."

The duke only grinned and shook his head.

"Our parents must be wondering what's happened to us, so it's time for us to be getting back now," Lisa informed him.

"Sorry about that," the duke said, "but you can't go. If you try to leave, you'll run into the cloak of invisibility on the far side of the moat, and that will stop you. I'm afraid you're trapped here unless you find the crystal ball."

"That's not fair!" Lisa protested. "We didn't ask to try to do something nobody else could do."

"But you came to the castle," the duke pointed out. "Sprod made the rules for people who come, and fairness depends on who makes the rules."

"No it doesn't," Cap argued. He couldn't deny that they had been warned against entering the castle. He could think of no way to call for help, but he still hoped to get out of the dangerous mess they were in. "Fair is fair. No one should have to take a big chance he didn't ask to take."

The duke sighed and said, "You're wasting time. If I were you, I'd get a move on."

"I'll help," Bounce offered. "I haven't had any luck before, but I know my way around the castle."

"I don't know why you're carrying a net," the duke said to Lisa. "Why not leave it here? It might get in your way."

Lisa looked at Cap and shrugged. He rolled his eyes and shrugged back. There seemed nothing left to do.

"I don't suppose anyone's likely to walk off

with it," Lisa remarked, propping her butterfly net against the arm of a woman too stiff to object.

Cap stared at the men and women who stood in the duke's grand hall without breathing. "These people looked everywhere before Sprod enchanted them. Where can we look that's new?"

"There are two places they probably didn't look," Lisa reasoned. "One is Lady Thistle's secret room, because they couldn't find it. The other is the dungeon, because it's guarded by the Baggish monster."

"Do we vote?" Bounce asked. "I don't think we should fool around with the monster."

"I'm sure that Thistle's secret room is in the tower on her side of the castle," Duke Lothrio said. "Sometimes I think I hear her singing to the birds at dawn."

"We ought to visit Sprod, the wizard," Cap said. "We can ask him for advice."

"And ask him please not to turn us into toads," Lisa added. "Maybe if we're polite—" She and Cap had both learned long ago that they were more likely to get what they wanted by asking nicely than by yelling.

Bounce led them up a long flight of stone

steps that wound around and around the inner-most part of the north tower. Twice he tripped and tumbled onto his hands and knees, but he jumped right up each time. "Falls don't hurt me," he said. "I always bounce back."

High in the tower, Cap and Lisa and Bounce came to a landing with a door. A sign on the door read: SPROD. BY APPOINTMENT ONLY. Next to the sign, a large iron ring dangled at the end of a chain.

"We don't have an appointment," said Cap, "but here goes."

He yanked the ring, and a bell rang inside. After a minute the door opened. A man wearing a long green robe and a hat as green and flat as a lime pie peered at them through square-rimmed glasses. Whiskers as long as broom bristles covered most of his face. "Ah, fresh eyes," he greeted the children.

"You must be Sprod, the famous wizard," Cap spoke up. "May we have an appointment?"

"That depends. When do you want one?"

"How about right now?"

"Let's see. I'm working on a spell to turn broccoli into plum pudding, and it's not going well. It's very hard to enchant broccoli or anything that's green. That's why I wear a green robe—I have enemies everywhere. I suppose there's no hurry. The best part of a problem is figuring out how to solve it. Yes, you can have an appointment now. Come in, come in."

We'd better find something green to wear in case we don't find the crystal ball, Cap thought to himself. Maybe we can string broccoli into chains and drape them around us.

When Sprod led the little group into his reception room, they saw the golden spell sprinkler and one petrified bat on their shelves in the display case. Another shelf was empty.

Several toads on the floor were playing leap toad, hopping across each other's backs. Six others were catching flies. A lump of sugar lay on the floor beneath a window, and the flies were buzzing around it. The toads waited in an orderly line, letting the first one catch a fly before the next one took its place. These were plainly toads who, in better days, had learned to take turns. If you liked toads, they weren't bad-looking, Cap thought, because instead of the usual dusty brown or green, their skins were violet and had rosy warts. But only a toad would want rosy warts.

Lisa looked from the toads back to Sprod.

"I had no idea wizards were so handsome," she said, sounding as if she meant it.

"Oh, do you think so?" Sprod picked up a mirror and stared at his reflection, turning his face from side to side. "You don't think my left eye squints too much?" He took off his glasses and considered the change in his appearance. "No, I think the glasses add character." He slipped them back on. "Actually, if I combed my whiskers and remembered to keep my back straight, I might cut a rather fine figure." He stared at Lisa and said, "You're a very perceptive young lady. What's your name?"

"I'm Lisa, and this is my brother, Cap. I guess you know Bounce."

"And you're going to find my crystal ball, aren't you? I never know whom my spell will bring."

"The spell worked fine," Lisa said, "but I do hope you won't think we have to be turned into toads and eat flies."

"Eating flies is no worse than eating broccoli three times a day, day after day. How I wish we had some tomato plants or carrot seeds! That's one thing I forgot about when I cast my spells. If you don't have a taste for flies, just find my crystal ball."

"We'll try," Cap said, "but you're the one who wants it. You should help. Lisa guessed that nobody looked in Lady Thistle's secret room because they couldn't find it. Can you tell us where it is?"

"Not without my crystal ball, I can't."

"Can't you give us any help at all?" Lisa asked in despair.

"Of course I can. I can give you some fortune cookies. They're full of useful hints."

Cap gestured toward the toads on the floor. "I suppose they got fortune cookies too."

"Yes, but they couldn't figure theirs out. The magic fortunes are like riddles." Sprod went into his laboratory and returned with his brown cookie jar. "You take one first," he said, offering the jar to Bounce.

Bounce pulled out a cookie, broke it open, and unfolded the slip of paper. *"Some secrets are twins,"* he read aloud. "How does that help?"

Sprod shook a finger at him sternly and said, "My fortune cookies always give excellent advice if you know how to take it."

Lisa took a cookie next. *"Every room has a door,"* she read. "Big deal. Everybody knows that."

"There must be a secret meaning," Sprod declared.

Then it was Cap's turn. He cracked a cookie open. *"Fire and ice don't mix,"* he read aloud. Trying to make sense out of it, he said, "I've seen fire around here—the torches on the walls—but where's the ice?"

"Take it from me, the fortune will prove useful if you're sharp enough," Sprod assured him.

"These cookies are good," Lisa remarked, finishing hers. "May we have some more, please?" She hoped she would get at least one simple, helpful message.

Sprod peered into the jar. "Yes. There are more here. You first, young lady."

Lisa's fortune was *Be brave to do good.* She shook her head in bafflement.

"Notice that it says *do good,* not *do well,*" Sprod pointed out. "Fortune cookies say exactly what they mean. It doesn't say *Be brave to excel.* It says you can do something good for someone if you aren't afraid."

Sprod gave Bounce the next cookie. *"Now you see it, now you don't,"* Bounce read. "Does that mean I'll find the crystal ball without even knowing it?"

Cap took the final cookie. *"Keep an eye on ups and downs,"* he read, thinking grumpily that it sounded like advice that Bounce could use. Cap was so disgusted that he crumbled the cookie and tossed the crumbs to the toads. They hopped about eagerly, flicking their long tongues in and out.

"You have a kind heart, young man," Sprod said with approval. "Even toads like an occasional treat. Now off with you. Happy hunting."

Bounce turned around to go and bumped into a chair. Down he fell. "Oh, that was funny," Sprod said, laughing. "Do it again."

"I only do it by accident," Bounce told him, bouncing to his feet with as much dignity as he could manage.

7

The Ghost
of Grung

"I don't see how the messages in the fortune cookies will help," Lisa said. "They haven't helped anyone else, and Sprod hasn't been able to find the crystal ball himself. I think he'd rather have more toads."

Lisa and Cap and Bounce were standing outside Sprod's door.

"Well," Cap observed with determination, "we can't wander around hoping we'll be lucky. We have to think."

"It's hard to think," Bounce said. "I never was very good at it."

"I still believe we should try to find Lady Thistle's secret room," Lisa said thoughtfully. "There's probably a secret passage to get to it.

Duke Lothrio said she went into her regular room, but nobody could find her there, so maybe she entered a secret passage from her room."

Bounce stared at Lisa with awe. "I'll bet if you were Sprod you could figure out how to turn broccoli into plum pudding."

"Or pizza," Cap said. "She's pretty smart. Let's go."

"What's pizza?" Bounce asked as they hurried down the winding steps of Sprod's tower.

"A big flat pie with cheese and stuff on top," Cap answered.

"Some people will eat anything," Bounce said, shaking his head as Cap led the way into the grand hall.

Duke Lothrio gave them a wave. "I'll bet Sprod gave you lots of good advice."

"No," said Cap.

"No," said Lisa.

"No," said Bounce. "Just some dumb fortunes."

"Oh," said the duke. "Well, tallyho!"

Bounce led them up a stairway to Thistle's room on the second floor near the south tower. He knocked on the door, and when there was no answer, pushed it open. Narrow oak panels carved with flowers lined the walls of the room. Paintings of cardinals, blue jays, orioles, and other colorful birds hung between the panels. The room had a feather bed, as Bounce discovered by sinking into it when he tried to bounce on it.

"In books and movies you always get into a secret passage by pushing a button that releases a hidden spring," Lisa said.

"What are movies?" Bounce asked.

"A lot of pictures that come one after another so fast that you think they're moving," she explained. "We should run our hands over everything and push and prod to find the spring."

Cap and Lisa and Bounce each took a wall. They ran their fingers along the edges of the panels and the carvings, paying particular attention to any small bumps that might be buttons. Cap unfolded the blade of his pocketknife to pry up a piece of loose wood. There was nothing but more wood underneath it. They felt along the edges of the paintings too.

"I'll try the closet," Lisa said. She ducked into a cubicle and began to look behind the dresses that hung on pegs.

A minute later Cap heard a yelp. He

stepped into the closet and found it empty. "Lisa!" he shouted.

There was a loud rapping behind a wall.

"Lisa, are you there?"

"Mmmph, rmmph."

"Come over here, Bounce," Cap called. "I think Lisa stepped through a door and got trapped somewhere." He rapped on the wall to let Lisa know he had heard her. "Bring a torch, Bounce. It's dark in here."

Bounce took a torch from its wall bracket and found flint and steel in a small box on top of Thistle's dresser. He struck sparks into the oil-soaked rushes. Flames sprang up and burned steadily as he carried the torch into the closet.

Cap felt for something that might work a hidden spring. He tugged at all of the clothes pegs, ending with the one nearest the door.

A slender panel, just wide enough for a person to slip through, swung backward silently from the closet wall. Lisa jumped through the opening into the closet and hugged Cap hard.

"Am I glad to be out of there!" she exclaimed with relief. "The door shut behind me when I went through, and it's darker than a black cat in there. I couldn't see a thing."

Cap watched the panel swing shut by itself,

as if his pulling the peg once had triggered a mechanism that both opened and closed the narrow door. "There has to be a way for people in there to get out. Bounce, will you bring me a chair?"

Bounce handed Lisa the torch and dragged over a chair that had gracefully curved legs and a rounded back. Cap pulled the clothes peg and wedged the chair into the doorway as the secret panel swung open. When the panel started to close, it was blocked by the chair.

"I'll go in and look for something that opens it from the inside," Cap said. He climbed over the chair and found himself in a dark, cold passageway. By the light of the torch Cap could see stone walls on both sides. They were so close together that he could stretch out his arms and touch both walls at once. At the end of the passageway he could make out stone steps.

Cap looked around and discovered a peg, like the one inside the closet, attached to the doorframe. When he pulled it, the panel swung back away from the chair.

To be sure of how it worked, he had Lisa hand him the torch and asked Bounce to take the chair out of the way. The panel closed, and he was alone in the passageway. He tugged at the peg, and the panel swung open.

"All right, it works both ways," he said. "We can explore the stairs now. I'll carry the torch and go first. Bounce, you can bring the flint and steel in case the torch goes out and we have to light it again."

The three of them squeezed into the passageway. "There are a lot of cobwebs, and the floor is covered with dust," Bounce observed. "Do you see all those marks in the dust? They look like footprints, but whose would they be?"

"Footprints would last a long time in dust that nobody swept," Cap said. Then he thought of another possibility. "If Thistle's secret room is up this way, maybe she comes down to her regular room sometimes."

Lisa edged past Cap. "Let me go first. I found the secret passage, so I get to find the secret room."

As she started up the steps at the far end of the passageway, something greenish gray and shimmering drifted through one wall and settled in front of her. Lisa stopped as the smoky apparition solidified in the shape of a knight in armor holding his head under one arm. A gust of icy air seemed to blow over her. She yelped and shrank back, bumping into Cap, who bumped into Bounce, who fell down.

They all looked at the frightening figure.

"Excuse me, sir," Bounce said shakily. "Are you a ghost?"

"What do you think I am, a mashed potato?" the head replied indignantly, nestled in the crook of the knight's elbow. "I am pleased to inform you that I am none other than the ghost of Sir Grung!"

"I'm afraid I didn't recognize you with your head down there," Bounce apologized as he stood up.

"You never were too bright. That stupid oaf Baggish sliced it off, remember? Do you think I would leave it to roll around on the floor all by itself?"

"I didn't know you had become a ghost. Why haven't the duke and I seen you before?"

"Because I have fun ruining the duke's chess games by moving the pieces around when he isn't looking, and I don't want him to see me. I've been waiting for you to learn to juggle well enough that I can snatch the balls out of the air and mix you up. But so far you get mixed up on your own."

"Have you tried putting your head back on?" Cap asked.

"Of course I have. I'm a very smart ghost. Watch." Grung took his head in both hands and placed it on his neck. It rested there as long as he didn't move, but when he nodded his head it slipped off. He had to catch it as it fell.

"It's safer this way," Grung said, cradling it again. "Besides, it's my second best trick. Ghosts who carry their heads under their arms are supposed to scare people witless. Why aren't you all cowering on the floor with your hands over your eyes, screaming for mercy?"

"Because the more you talk, the safer we feel." Cap wasn't scared; he was curious. "What's your best trick?"

"Grabbing people and freezing them with a grip of ice!"

Cap thought of the first fortune he had received: *Fire and ice don't mix.* Maybe it had something to do with the ghost.

Grung raised his head high in the air with one hand and yelled, "Eee-yah!" He leaped forward and seized Lisa's arm.

"Let go!" she cried out as icy cold shot through her arm from her hand to her shoul-

der. "Your hand is like dry ice! It's freezing me!"

Cap thrust his torch at the ghost's body. It let go of Lisa and backed away. Shreds of vapor swirled into the air and then drifted back into place.

"We don't have to be afraid of you," Cap said. "Fire and ice don't mix! You melt!"

"That's what you think," Grung sneered. "Fire stirs up my ectoplasm, the way wind blows clouds apart, but it only takes a minute for me to readjust. I'm ready to go again. I'll get you when you're not looking!"

Bounce was quivering with curiosity. "Excuse me, sir," he said again, "but I thought ghosts hung around at night and didn't come out in the daytime. How come, I mean why are you doing ghost stuff during the day?"

"Who told you that ghosts don't come out in the daytime? We can appear anytime we want to. But sunlight is so bright that people can't see us, so we can't scare them. In here it's dark enough for you to see me, even with that stinking torch. Don't give me any more trouble. Run! Yell for help!"

"Some other time, maybe," Cap said. He knew he didn't have to run while he had a torch. "We're looking for Lady Thistle's secret room. Do you know where that is?"

"Of course I do. I know where everything in the castle is."

"I bet you don't know where Sprod's crystal ball is," Lisa challenged him.

"What do you mean I don't know? I'm the one who hid it."

"I'll believe you if you show it to us," Lisa said.

The ghost of Grung laughed nastily, gurgling and snorting as if he were swallowing soup. "You can't catch me with that trick, stupid. I'm too smart. But I'll give you a hint. Sometimes it's in plain sight. That's the cleverest way to hide something."

Cap thought of Bounce's fortune: *Now you see it, now you don't.* A place that was hidden in the dark of night but was in plain sight in daylight would fit. But that was no help because every place in the castle was dark at night.

"Do you know what Sprod will do to us if we don't find his crystal ball?" Cap asked.

"You bet I do. It's fun to watch. Too bad, kiddies. You're headed for toad time. That may be the best thing that could happen to you because I don't bother toads. Hee, hurgle, hee!

Ha, harrup, ha!" The ghost made his soup-swallowing sounds again.

Somehow a nasty laugh sounded nastier when it came from near the elbow.

"It wouldn't hurt to tell us where Thistle's secret room is," Bounce said. "Would you be kind enough to do that, sir?"

"I wouldn't be kind enough to give water to a fish. I'm mean and I hate everybody, especially since Lady Thistle won't marry me. She should have said yes after I told her how smart I was." The ghost struck his breastplate with a gauntleted hand. When the clanging died down, he said, "Forsooth, anon!"

"What's that mean?" Cap asked.

"*Forsooth* means you'd better believe it. *Anon* means I'll see you later, garlic grater." With that, the ghost drifted back through the wall.

"Let's go," Cap said. "I'll keep my torch ready. Forsooth! Grung is going to be a big pain in the neck."

Lisa led the way up the steps, which wound around, higher and higher, from one landing to another. "We must be in the tower by now," she said.

"Yah! Gotcha!" a voice yelled. Grung's ghost had slipped up behind Bounce and grabbed him by the neck. Bounce tripped and fell. He looked as if he were strangling in a grip of ice, but Cap leaped back and drove the ghost away with his torch.

"Stop bothering us!" Cap shouted. "I'll cook you until you boil away."

"Big words!" the ghost scoffed. "See you later, baked pertater." And he disappeared again.

Bounce bounced to his feet, and the friends continued upward until the steps ended in a final landing. A door was set in the wall. Lisa ran to it and knocked. When she heard no answer, she pulled the door open.

She found herself on a small balcony, staring across a railing at the forest beyond the castle. She craned her neck upward and saw the top of the tower not far above her. Birds were flying around it.

"This is just a lookout place," she said with disappointment. "I don't see a window near me. Maybe the secret room is on the other side of the tower. If I call to Lady Thistle, she might hear. Lady Thistle! Lady Thistle!"

There was no answer. Discouraged, Lisa returned to the little landing. Cap and Bounce took turns on the balcony but saw no more than she had.

"The tower is wide enough for a secret

room," Cap said. "Let's look for a button to open a secret door."

They felt all around the landing, pushing against every stone, but nothing happened.

"There's something funny about this," Cap observed. "Nobody would need a secret passage to go to a lookout balcony. If there's a secret room up here, there must be a trick to finding it that we haven't figured out." He stared at the floor and wondered what to do next. Sometimes when his soccer team was behind, he would call his teammates together to change tactics. Sometimes it worked.

"One of our fortunes said *Some secrets are twins,* and another said *Keep an eye on ups and downs,*" he reminded Bounce and Lisa. "The towers of the castle are twins, and we've been climbing up and down them, but maybe not far enough. Where is the dungeon, Bounce?"

"Below Sprod's tower."

"Let's go down there," Lisa urged. "We can all carry torches to drive the ghost and the monster off if we have to. Maybe the crystal ball is down there. Anyway, the monster used to be Sir Baggish, you know. I'll bet he knows how to get to Thistle's secret room."

8

Encounter with
a Monster

Back down the secret passage
they went, out through the
closet, through the room that
Thistle used when she wasn't
hiding, and down to the grand
reception hall. The duke
looked at their grim faces and said, "No luck
so far, eh?"

"No," Cap answered. "All we found was a
secret passage and a ghost."

"Then you must be doing very well in-
deed," the duke said. "I didn't know we had a
secret passage in the castle. And what a happy
surprise to learn we have a ghost! It gives a
castle special standing to have a ghost, you
know. When this business is all over, I can in-

vite a lot of people who have castles without ghosts to come over and see mine. Whose ghost is it, by the way?"

"Sir Grung's," Lisa answered. "I don't think he's a party ghost. He clanks his armor, and he carries his head in one arm, and he tries to grab people and freeze them with an icy grip."

The duke shook his head sadly. "Sounds like Grung all right. Too bad. I never knew a lady of good breeding who liked an icy grip. How did you escape being frozen?"

"With a torch," Cap answered. "Fire shakes him up. Keep a lot of torches handy if you have a party. Grung will come whether you invite him or not."

"Now we're going to see the monster," Lisa explained.

"I wouldn't go near him if I were you," the duke said. "He's tied to an iron ring at the top of the dungeon steps, but he can still scuttle around the corridor. If I ever want to put any prisoners in the dungeon, I don't know how I'll slip them past him. Sometimes I think Sprod's spell was sloppy at the corners."

"We'll watch out," Cap promised.

"Be careful not to fall into the food hole,"

the duke added. "It's a chute for dropping food to prisoners. We drop a barrel of cider to them on holidays, if we have prisoners and remember to do it. The hole is near the entrance to the corridor."

At last the duke had given them some useful advice, Cap thought. Lisa and Bounce took two more torches from the walls, and Cap followed them as Bounce led the way toward the dungeon. In a few moments, they reached a narrow corridor between damp stone walls and saw the food hole to one side. It gaped wide, without a railing around it.

Beyond the hole, in front of steps that led farther down, the monster waited, watching.

It looked more frightful than they had imagined. Its eyes gleamed red. Its teeth gleamed ivory. Its jaws were wide enough to swallow one of them in a single gulp. It smelled worse than moldy goat cheese. It smelled like moldy mold.

"Ee-ee-ee yah!" something screeched. The ghost of Grung had filtered through a wall and was holding his head high in one hand while he reached for Bounce with the other. Bounce jumped to get away, but he tripped and fell forward. With a wail, he disappeared down the food hole headfirst. His torch scraped along the side of the chute and went out.

"Ah, harrup, ah, harrup!" The ghost laughed his slurpy laugh. "Ho ho, hurgle, and another harrup! That fixes one of you. Who'll be next? See you later, fishhook baiter." The ghost vanished through the wall.

Lisa knelt and called down the food hole. "Bounce, are you hurt?"

"No," Bounce called back. His voice echoed along the hollow chute. "I landed on a pile of straw."

"We'll get you out," Cap shouted. "I'll go back up and find a rope and lower it to you."

"That . . . won't . . . be . . . necebbary . . . I mean . . . necessary," a deep voice said slowly. It was the monster speaking, sounding like a tuba. "He . . . can crumb . . . come . . . this way."

"Oh, sure," Cap said sarcastically. "And let you eat Bounce?"

"Oh . . . just a bite . . . to see what . . . beeble . . . I mean, people . . . taste like. I've never . . . had a chance to beat . . . eat . . . anyone before. Every day the book . . . um, crook . . . no, cook . . . comes and shoves . . . a crate . . . um, plate . . . of brobboli at me.

Monsters are subbosed . . . to gubble down beeple. Excuse my peach . . . I mean, my speech. I haven't . . . practiced for so long. Nobubble ever comes . . . to tell me anything. Have your friend . . . come up past me. I promise to . . . take only a fright. A kite? A bite!"

"No way," Cap said.

"Not even a nubble? Norble? Nibble! Tell him the boast . . . rather, the roast . . . um, the coast is clear."

Lisa was staring hard at the monster. It was the ugliest, scariest thing she had ever seen. She wondered if Lady Thistle would have been willing to kiss it. The thought of coming within reach of those sharp claws and long teeth and that awful smell made her close her eyes and shiver.

"What's going on up there?" Bounce called through the food hole. "Did you get the rope? It's as dark as the inside of a potato cellar down here. I can feel stone walls and steps going up, but I can't see a thing. I'm getting scared."

"Did you drop your flint and steel?" Cap called. "If you still have them, light your torch."

"I'm not sure I can do it in the dark."
Bounce grew silent for a moment. "There. I
did it!" he shouted. "It's going great! Oh, no!
The pile of straw's on fire! A spark must have
hit it! I'll burn up! I'll have to try to get out
past the monster!"

Smoke began pouring out of the food hole
and up the steps. Cap and Lisa knew that
smoke was as dangerous as fire because a person could smother in it.

The monster scurried to the top of the steps
and licked its teeth greedily. "Ah! Boasted toy
. . . I mean, toasted boy! Yum!"

Lisa could see Bounce's head near the top
of the steps. He was coughing from the smoke.
"Don't come any closer!" she called to him.
"Back away! Lie down and breathe the air near
the floor! Smoke rises! It will go over your
head!"

Bounce backed down the steps—too late.
The monster reached out with a foreleg and
hooked its claws in Bounce's shirt. "He got
me!" Bounce yelled. "And it's my best shirt,
too. He's pulling me toward his teeth! Help!"

Cap and Lisa heard thumps and the sound
of boots scraping on stone as Bounce struggled.
Then the monster backed toward them, and

they could see that it was dragging Bounce with it.

"Stop wiggling," the monster said. "Be a good little dinner."

"Baggish!" Bounce cried. "Don't you remember me? I'm Bounce, the court juggler. We were friends!"

"Those were the old good days . . . the good old days, were they? Too bad I don't rememble, but it's really grape . . . I mean, great to see you. We'll celebrate with a beast . . . um, a feast. You look suspicious . . . I mean, delicious."

Cap saw that the monster was giving its full attention to Bounce, so he held out his torch and sneaked forward. When he came close, he threw the torch, and it landed under the monster's tail.

"Yeeow!" the monster screeched. It whirled around, releasing Bounce, who scrambled back down the steps into the dungeon. The monster thwacked its tail on the stone floor to put out sparks and kicked the torch back at Cap.

Cap dodged and picked it up again.

"I'm in the dungeon, but I'm all right now," Bounce called up. "Straw burns fast, and the smoke is almost gone."

The monster looked at Cap and said, "Burning my tail was a dirty brick . . . I mean, trick."

"Eating Bounce would be a dirtier trick."

"Eat him? Me? I promised not to, didn't I? You sound like a mine young fan . . . I mean, fine young man, not the kind who would suspect an honest monster. Come closer so I can fake . . . um, take . . . a better look at you."

Cap wondered how far the monster's rope extended. "We're close enough," he said.

The monster tried to smile. It looked like a toothpaste ad for rats. "Let's be pals," it said in its deep voice. "I know how to be rice . . . ah, nice. I wasn't always a monster, you know. Once I was Sir Grabbish—no, Sir Rubbish—no, that's not it, either—Sir Baggish, just as my wiggly young friend said. I was the bride . . . pride . . . of the duke's court. I never thought of eating anyone. Even now I would rather eat . . . brobboli? . . . than beople. What could be tastier than brobboli on a bed of spinach, sprinkled with grated turnips? There's no law that says a monster can't be a veterinarian . . . I mean, a vegetarian."

"Do you remember Lady Thistle?" Lisa asked.

"Lady Whistle? No. Lady Bristle? Hmmm. Oh, Lady Thistle! Now that I think of it, I resemble her . . . um, remember her. I made up bonnets . . . I mean, sonnets for her. She had just enough fat to make her tender and juicy. Uh, that is, she was just plump enough to make a perfect fife—I mean wife. She would have been mine if that wizard, Clod—no, Scrod—no, Sprod, that's it—hadn't given me this nice squat scaly shape. I wonder why she never comes to see me."

"Because she's waiting for you to come to her. She got mad when Sprod enchanted you, and she hid in her secret room. Do you know where it is?"

"Let's see. I don't think I knew she had a secret room."

"If we found Lady Thistle, she could kiss you to end the enchantment and turn you back into Sir Baggish," Lisa said.

"What! And boil me . . . I mean, spoil the way I am? I'll have to think that over." The monster cocked its head at them. "Let me see . . . If she did that, I could bury her . . . um, marry her instead of eating her, couldn't I? I'll tell you what." It scraped the stone floor eagerly with its claws. "You untie me, and we'll all go looking for her secret room together."

Lisa took a giant step backward. "You might forget you had decided to be a vegetarian," she said. "How do we know you won't eat us?"

The monster took a giant step forward. "Pish, tush! Say! I just remembered where Thistle's secret room is. But we have to keep it a secret. Come here, and I'll whimper . . . whisper it in your ear."

What a liar, Cap thought in disgust. And a dumb one, too. "Come on, Lisa," he said. "Let's go find a rope for Bounce."

But as Cap turned, he saw what looked like smoke collecting near a wall. Suddenly the smoke took shape as the ghost of Grung. Before Cap could raise his torch, the ghost shouted "Gotcha!" and gave him a hard shove toward the monster.

The monster rushed forward.

Cap saw broad jaws open wide for him. He kicked out, but his shoe skidded off the monster's slippery scales. Down he fell, and the monster snagged his jeans with its claws. Cap swung his torch at the monster's head, but the monster lashed its tail around like a heavy whip to knock the torch away.

"At last!" the monster bellowed. "What a nice change from brobboli! You are dumbed! I mean, doomed!" Its blood-red tongue snaked over its gleaming teeth. "Let's see. Shall I nubble a pinkie first? I mustn't eat you too fast. I don't want a dummy ache."

"No!" Cap yelled. He struggled to break free, but the monster pulled him in. "Let go! Lisa, help!"

Lisa took a step forward. She felt ready to cry in fear and disgust at the thought of doing the only thing that would save her brother.

Cap, kicking and squirming, looked at her desperately. "Hurry!" he cried.

Lisa held her nose against the smell, closed her eyes, and puckered her lips. Then she dove forward toward the loathsome creature.

9

Secret Hiding Places

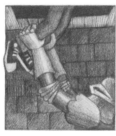

When Lisa opened her eyes, she was sitting on the floor, staring up at a tall knight in armor. A rope around his neck led to an iron ring in the wall. The knight was holding Cap upside down by one leg and looked ready to bite Cap's foot.

The knight looked around, frowning, as if puzzled by where he was and what he was doing. "Kindly remove your foot from my face, boy. It's not polite," he said.

"Set me down, please," Cap asked in a shaky voice. He was trembling. When the knight turned him upright and lowered him gently to the floor, Cap felt a surge of relief that he was safe. "Thanks, Lisa," he said. "You were braver than anybody I ever heard of. You're a hero! You saved my life." He helped her up from the floor and gave her a hug.

"I couldn't bear to see anything bad happen to you," she said. Wiping her lips, she added, "What a slimy taste!"

"This girl saved your life?" the knight asked. "I am supposed to be the hero around here. I am Sir Baggish the basher."

"But you wouldn't have saved anybody's life. You were the danger," Cap said. "Sprod turned you into a monster. Lisa kissed you and released you from Sprod's spell just when you were about to eat me."

"Eat you? Ho, ho, ho! You can't expect me to believe that!"

"Look. You're still tied to the wall. Think about it."

Baggish turned and fingered the rope. "Very strange," he said. "I seem to remember Sprod having something to do with that. Yes, it's coming back to me. I spent a lot of time crawling around. But did I really want to eat people? Ugh! I owe you thanks too, Lisa. You saved me from unthinkable disgrace."

"That's all right," Lisa said, blushing with embarrassment. Then she grinned. "We heroes have to stick together."

"I'll cut you loose," Cap offered, and did so with his knife.

"All this namby-pamby goody-goody stuff!" someone said. It was the ghost of Grung, whom the others had forgotten. He was hopping from one vaporous armored foot to the other in fury. Cap hurriedly recovered his torch.

"Don't think you've seen the last of me!" Grung shouted. "By doing Baggish a favor, you've made me as mad as ten swarms of hornets. You can't foil me forever. Forsooth, anon! See you later, garbage freighter." He filtered through a wall.

"That was Grung, wasn't it?" Baggish said. "He's looking a little pale these days. As rude as ever, though, vanishing like that. Did you notice that his head seems to be mixed up with his elbow? Now that I think about it, I seem to remember cutting his head off. Yes. Quite by accident, I assure you, in a little fight over Lady Thistle. Thistle! I can't wait to see her!"

"We've been trying to find her secret room," Cap said. "We need to keep looking, but first we have to get Bounce out of the dungeon and see if Sprod's crystal ball is down there. You wanted to eat Bounce too."

Sir Baggish shook his head remorsefully.

"Being turned into a monster ruins one's character."

Cap held his torch and led the way down the dungeon steps. There was Bounce, sitting on the stone floor, his chin resting on one hand.

"Boy, am I glad to see you!" Bounce exclaimed. "I heard a lot of noise up there, and it worried me. And Sir Baggish! You were such an evil monster you would have scared yourself."

"This young lady disenchanted me with a kiss without bothering about how I could bite her head off," Baggish said.

"Do you know what?" Bounce asked. "That was in your fortune cookie, Lisa. *Be brave to do good.* You were brave to kiss the monster, and you did good by changing Sir Baggish back to a knight and making it possible for me to get out of the dungeon."

"He's right," Cap agreed. "We've figured out another fortune. Now let's see if the crystal ball is hidden down here." He pushed ashes aside and held his torch in every corner, but there was no sign of the crystal ball.

"While I was down here," Bounce said, "I was thinking. One of my fortune cookies said

Some secrets are twins. The castle towers are twins, but they aren't secret because everyone can see them. We couldn't find Thistle's room by following the secret passage, but what if she has a secret passage off her secret passage? Twin secret passages!"

"Don't tell *me* it's hard for you to think," Cap said. "Let's try it."

On the way back to Thistle's regular room, they passed through the grand reception hall again. Duke Lothrio rose from his chair in amazement. "Baggish, my boy!" he exclaimed. "What a nice surprise! I thought Sprod had fixed you for good. How come, I mean, why— sloppy talk must be contagious, but that's neither here nor there, now, is it?—why aren't you a monster?"

"This brave girl changed me back with a kiss." Sir Baggish patted Lisa on the head, very gently so as not to bash her with the steel gauntlet on his hand. "Now we're off to find Lady Thistle's secret room so I can marry her. I have to find her first."

"Right," the duke agreed. "It seems to me, though, that it might be wise to find the stolen crystal ball first, so Sprod doesn't change this brave little girl and her brother into toads."

"Maybe he'll let us go because we saved Sir Baggish," Lisa said in a hopeful voice.

"Not Sprod. Once he makes up his mind, he won't change it for a wagonload of petrified bats."

"We think the crystal ball may be hidden in Thistle's secret room," Cap said.

The duke frowned and shook his head. "Maybe so, but if the crystal ball was in Thistle's room, she would have found it and brought it out, wouldn't she?"

"Maybe it's hidden so well, she doesn't know it's there," Lisa suggested.

"If that's the case, you'd better find her soon." The duke waggled a finger at them. "Sprod is a very impatient wizard."

Cap and Lisa and Bounce led Baggish to the secret passageway off Thistle's regular room. When they came to the foot of the steps leading to the top of the tower, Cap stopped.

"It's no use going up to the landing," he said. "We searched everywhere up there. Let's check the passageway here before it reaches the steps. Push every stone. Press all the cracks."

Baggish thrust the point of his sword into cracks and seams in the walls, and Cap slid his knife along them, but nothing happened. Lisa and Bounce kicked the lower stones and pushed the higher ones. One thing did happen. Their toes hurt.

Cap gazed upward, wondering about a trapdoor. Spiderwebs crossed the ceiling. Most of them were thick and tangled and dusty, but in one corner there was a squarish space where they were thin and patchy.

"Sir Baggish, lift me up there, will you?" Cap asked, pointing. "I want to take a closer look. Hold my torch, Lisa."

Baggish lifted Cap onto his shoulders. Cap had to duck his head to keep from bumping the ceiling. There, where the cobwebs were thin, he saw a square of wood, not stone. He pushed, and the square swung up and back.

"It's a trapdoor!" he shouted.

Baggish held Cap by the ankles and boosted him through the opening, then passed up a torch.

Cap found himself in another stone hallway. "It's a secret passage off the secret passage," he called. "Come on up, and we'll see where it goes."

"How could Thistle ever get up there?" Bounce asked.

"Maybe she kept a ladder in her closet,"

Lisa answered. "She could have used it to climb through the trapdoor, then dragged the ladder up behind her so she could climb down again."

Baggish lifted Lisa and Bounce up, and Cap took their torches and helped pull them through the trapdoor. That left Baggish. To his dismay, he discovered that, with his heavy armor on, he couldn't jump much higher than a turtle, not nearly high enough to reach the opening. Each time he tried it, he came down in a clatter of steel plates.

"If you find Lady Thistle and she has a ladder, bring it to me," Baggish said. "Tell her I'm eagerly waiting to rescue her."

We're the ones who are doing the rescuing, Cap thought, but he didn't argue. He told Bounce to drop his torch to Baggish so that the knight wouldn't be left in the dark. Baggish caught it deftly.

Just in time, too. The wall rippled and smoked, and the ghost of Grung materialized in front of Sir Baggish. "Try bashing me now, stupid!"

"Avaunt, wretched wraith!" Baggish shouted. "Begone!" He drew his sword and swung. The sword met no resistance but swept through the shimmering, pale vapor of the ghost without leaving a mark. Baggish whirled around like a top.

"Harrup, harrup!" Grung laughed. "I can turn solid when I want to grab people or turn misty when I want to escape. That's my third best trick. You made me into a ghost who has to carry his head around. Now you can see how you like it. I'm going to freeze your head off."

Grung seized the collar of steel around Baggish's neck. Baggish desperately swept his torch through the ghost, and the vapor disintegrated.

"I'll get you yet!" Grung vowed after he had pulled himself together. "See you later, teapot plater." He melted into the wall.

After watching Baggish drive off the ghost, Lisa ran down the secret passage off the secret passage with Cap and Bounce behind her. At the end, she found an ordinary door. "*Every room has a door,* my fortune said. I hope this door belongs to the room we're looking for."

As eager as she was to enter, she remembered to knock politely.

"Baggish?" a woman's voice called through the door.

"No. I'm Lisa. Are you Lady Thistle?"

"Of course I am. Where's Baggish?"

"He's waiting to rescue you."

The door opened, and Lisa saw before her a tall woman in a long blue dress embroidered with orange eggs. She stared at Cap and Bounce but didn't ask their names. The sound of birds chirping and twittering came through the doorway.

"What took Baggish so long, that's what I'd like to know," Thistle demanded.

"Well, for a long time he was a monster tied by a rope," Lisa answered.

"That's no excuse. I know he was a monster. Why didn't he escape and scare Sprod into changing him back? Why didn't he chew through the rope?"

"He wasn't a very smart monster. He probably didn't think of it. I guess nobody told you to go down and kiss him."

"What! Kiss that horrid thing! Why would I do that?"

"Because it would have ended the spell and turned him back into a knight."

Thistle's eyes widened. "Oh, no! I guess they didn't tell me because they couldn't find me. Where is Baggish now?"

"He's waiting for us to bring him your ladder."

Thistle laughed. "If Baggish thinks he's

going to rescue me, he has a surprise coming. I come and go whenever I want."

"You do?" Lisa exclaimed in surprise.

"Why shouldn't I? About three days after Sprod turned Baggish into a monster and I fled to my secret room, I grew tired of being a tragic heroine. I went down to the grand hall. Everybody was frozen stiff except my father, and he was too busy playing chess with himself to notice me. If he had seen me there, he would have expected me to play chess with him all day long, every day. It wouldn't have been any fun because whenever I beat him he claims I cheated. I decided I would rather weave tapestries of birds. Come in. I'll show you."

Birds were flying in and out of a small window as Cap and Lisa and Bounce entered Thistle's secret room. Birdhouses hung from the ceiling. Tapestries covered the walls and lay in piles on the floor. They were all woven in patterns of birds—tiny birds hatching from eggs; nestlings with their beaks wide open to be fed; birds snapping up insects and pecking for seeds; and large and small birds flying in the air. The tapestry on Thistle's loom showed a bird with a tall black and white crest.

"That's my hoopoe," Thistle explained.

"I'm weaving every bird in the world. When I whistle birdcalls, they come and pose for me. I reward them with seeds that I take from the garden when I go down to the kitchen at night for broccoli. Someday I plan to open a museum of bird tapestries."

Cap doubted that Thistle knew every kind of bird in the world. "Do you have a penguin tapestry?" he asked her.

"What's a penguin?"

"It's a black and white bird with flippers instead of wings. It swims instead of flying. It lives on ice at the bottom of the world and catches fish in the cold oceans there."

"At the bottom of the world? Do you mean it lives upside down?" Thistle asked.

"No, what looks upside down from here is right-side up down there," Cap answered.

Thistle narrowed her eyes. "You must be joking," she said. "Anyway, I'd like to see a penguin. Hmmm. Let's get Baggish."

She dragged her ladder out from behind her loom. Cap let it down through the trapdoor, and Baggish climbed up to join them.

Since the visor of his helmet was raised, Thistle could see his face. She smiled and said, "Welcome back from monsterhood. You're looking much better than the last time I saw you, scraping around on the floor."

"Thistle-whistle!" Baggish answered fondly, drawing her into his embrace. "At last!" He took his helmet off politely before kissing her.

"It's wonderful to see you again, Baggie dear!" Thistle said, wincing as Baggish clamped her against his steel breastplate. "Will you go on a quest for me?"

"To the very ends of the earth!"

"How did you guess! You're so clever! I want you to bring me a penguin."

"As soon as you tell me what it is."

"Can we look around first?" Cap asked impatiently. "We're hunting for Sprod's crystal ball, and we have to find it before he turns us into toads."

"Grung couldn't have hidden it here because he didn't know my secret room was here," Thistle said.

"Maybe he knew, and you didn't know he knew, and he knew you didn't know he knew," Cap replied.

Thistle glanced at Cap sharply and then nodded. "With Grung, you never know. Look around. I'll twitter while you work."

Cap and Lisa and Bounce searched high and

low. The boys held the ladder so Lisa could climb up and look inside the birdhouses. They looked under Thistle's bed and bedding, behind a chair and under its cushion, inside every drawer, inside the closet. They looked in every corner, around Thistle's loom, behind the tapestries hanging on the wall, and under the tapestries piled on the floor.

All the while, birds flew in and out the window as Thistle twittered and chirped and trilled. They circled the children's heads and swooped in front of their eyes. "I like the little flitty ones, don't you?" Thistle asked as a sparrow perched on Cap's shoulder.

Cap didn't answer. He thought that Thistle had birds on the brain. He stood up, discouraged because no matter where they looked, there was no crystal ball.

"We figured out the fortune about twin secrets, and that made the one about every room has a door come true," Bounce said. *"Fire and ice don't mix* drove Grung away, and *Be brave to do good* saved Cap and changed Baggish back. We have two fortunes left: *Now you see it, now you don't,* and *Keep an eye on ups and downs."*

Lisa had gone to the window to watch flocks of birds in the sky. "Ups and downs," she murmured. "We're up, so let's look down." She braced herself against the window ledge and leaned out. "It's a bird's-eye view. I can see the castle courtyard and the walls and moat. Wait!"

She turned to Cap with excitement. "We've looked inside the castle. How about outside? What if Grung hid the crystal ball somewhere on the outside of the castle?"

"That's a great idea," Cap said. "Let's go!"

10

Last Chance

Baggish carried Thistle's ladder for her without being asked and helped her through the trapdoor. As they walked downstairs, he was apparently trying to think up a brand new sonnet, for the others heard him say, "My Thistle's eyes are round as a wagon wheel. Uh, let's see. Da de da de da de da de da dum."

"Da de da de da de da de da dum," Thistle repeated with a grin. "That's a marvelous line!"

Baggish got no farther before they came to the grand hall.

Duke Lothrio glanced up. "Ah! You're just in time," he declared. "This very moment I beat myself in a chess game. It isn't easy, you know."

He was so busy congratulating himself that he didn't really notice who was there until Thistle said drily, "Perhaps you should give yourself a handicap."

"Thistle!" the duke exclaimed. "They found you. Wonderful!"

"I was never lost," Thistle remarked.

"If we couldn't find you, you must have been lost. Well, I'm glad to see you," said the duke. "Now you and Baggish and I can make plans for your wedding. Since the knights and ladies of my court still aren't showing any more zip than the shields that decorate my walls, Cap can be best man and Lisa can be maid of honor. Even if Sprod has turned you into toads by then. Toads at a wedding—there's a first time for everything! Wouldn't that be fun?"

"No," said Cap.

"No," said Lisa.

"I don't think they plan on being toads," said Bounce. "They're determined to find the crystal ball. We're going to look outside."

The drawbridge over the moat had been down ever since Cap and Lisa first crossed it. As they walked back over it with Bounce, he tripped on a plank that wasn't fitted smoothly to the others. Luckily, he caught himself before tumbling into the water.

At the far side of the drawbridge, they could see down the hill and across the valley to the forest. But when Cap and Lisa tried to walk toward the trees, on the chance that they might escape, they bumped into the cloak of invisibility that Sprod had created. They were forced to walk along the outer edge of the moat and continue their search.

"Bounce, you look down into the moat," Cap said. "It seems to be running water, and it's clear. Can you swim?"

"Like a bird," Bounce answered.

Cap was puzzled. "Like a bird? You mean a penguin?"

Bounce laughed. "Like a duck. I like to do acrobatics in the water because I never fall down. Except sometimes I get water up my nose."

"Well, if you see anything round and glassy, the size of two fists, dive down and fish it out," Cap said. "Lisa and I will walk around the moat and look across at the castle walls. If we see anything there, I'll have Baggish lower me from the battlements to inspect it."

Lisa and Cap walked along the narrow strip of land between the moat and the cloak of invisibility. The castle walls looked like nothing more than blocks of stone, all alike, all fitted together smoothly. There were no suspicious-looking bumps, no cracks or gaps where something could be hidden. The walls were gray and blank, featureless except for the battlements on top, with their openings for archers. These showed no sign of the crystal ball either. When Cap and Lisa had walked all the way around and were back where they had started, they saw Bounce bending over, peering into the moat. He had hardly moved six feet.

"He'll take forever," Lisa said. "Let's go around again and look into the moat ourselves."

The moat wasn't muddy at the bottom. It was scoured clean by water flowing swiftly from an unseen source to an unseen outlet. Silvery fishes swam in it, and black beetles skated across the surface. Snails crept along the bottom and sides. There were no rocks, no trash, and nothing that looked like a crystal ball, either.

As Cap and Lisa came back to the draw-bridge, they heard a splash. Bounce's head popped up a few yards out in the water. He started to dog-paddle toward shore, but the current caught him and swept him under the drawbridge.

Cap and Lisa heard a thud.

"Ow!" Bounce cried.

He emerged on the other side of the draw-bridge and swam to the bank, where Cap helped him climb out.

"I cracked my head hard under there," Bounce said, squeezing water out of his clothes. He touched the top of his head and winced. "It was dark, and I saw this black bump too late to duck. It's the first time I ever tripped on something above my head."

"Did you dive into the water because you thought you saw the crystal ball?" Cap asked.

"I didn't dive; I fell," Bounce answered sheepishly. "I leaned over too far and lost my balance. I need a towel and some dry clothes. Let's go back to the castle."

"We might as well. I can't think of any-thing else to do," Cap said dejectedly.

"Maybe we'll find a way to soften up Sprod," Lisa murmured quietly.

They walked slowly, reluctantly, across the drawbridge. As they entered the courtyard, they heard the creak of windlasses turning and the dull clank of iron chains. The drawbridge was being raised by an unseen power.

"Ah, there you are," Duke Lothrio said when Cap and Lisa and Bounce returned to the grand hall. He raised his eyebrows at the sight of Bounce dripping wet. "I suppose you heard the drawbridge close. A sad sound, I dare say. It means your time is up, I'm afraid. Sprod ought to be down any minute. I am sorry about all this. I want you to know that Lady Thistle and Sir Baggish and I will be eternally grateful for how you've helped us. We'll be sure to come visit you up in Sprod's room. Friends are a comfort when you're feeling like a toad. That's one of my wise sayings."

"It's all hot air, and you're just a windy old gasbag unless you have a wise saying that will help us get out of here," Cap flared, thinking only of being turned into a toad and not caring whom he insulted.

"Don't imagine talk like that will help you, young man," the duke said sternly. "I would be glad to free you from the spell if I could."

"I see we're all here," said another voice ominously. Sprod had entered the room without anyone noticing. He was carrying his golden spell sprinkler. "Have you searched everywhere? Did you use all the fortune cookies? It doesn't look like it. I don't see my crystal ball."

"Why don't you make the ghost of Grung tell you where it is?" Cap demanded. "He's the one who stole it and hid it, and he's been floating around here all the time. You could turn him into the ghost of a toad if he doesn't confess."

"True, but if he doesn't confess, that wouldn't get me my crystal ball, now, would it?"

"Maybe he'd rather be a headless ghost and go around trying to freeze people than be a wispy ghost of a toad," Cap said.

"You don't know Grung," Sprod replied. "He thinks it's a splendid joke to cause people trouble. Any kind of ghost can do that. If I turned him into the ghost of a toad, he would have his head on his neck again, but he could still scare people. Think of having a toad ghost hop onto your pillow at night! It's no use, young man. Let's get on with it." He raised his spell sprinkler and addressed Lisa. "Ladies first. What color toad would you like to be?"

"I don't want to be any color toad!" Lisa shouted at him. "You should help us, not hurt us! We tried to help you!"

"I did help. I gave you the fortune cookies. It's not my fault if you couldn't figure them out."

"We did figure out some of them," Lisa

shot back. "Doesn't it count that we helped Sir Baggish and Lady Thistle?"

"That's Duke Lothrio's affair, not mine. He can give you jewels. I don't mind if my toads have jewels."

Cap saw Lisa look around frantically. He thought he knew what she was hoping to find because he'd been looking for it too. But there wasn't a touch of green anywhere in the room, except for what Lothrio and Bounce and Sprod were wearing. Blue, yellow, red, brown, pink and purple, silver and gold adorned the tapestries and banners and shields, but no green. He and Lisa would be turned into toads, while Duke Lothrio remained the same and Bounce had only suffered a bruise on the head.

Probably a painful bruise, Cap thought, as he noticed Bounce touching it gingerly. As Cap looked at the goose egg that had risen on Bounce's head, he had the strange feeling that it ought to remind him of something. Bounce said he had seen a black bump that he couldn't dodge as he was swept under the drawbridge. He had banged his head on the bump, and then the current had carried him past it.

Cap's eyes widened. What had happened to Bounce would fit the fortune: *Now you see it, now you don't.*

But a crystal ball wouldn't be black.

Yes it would, Cap thought, if it was underneath a lowered drawbridge. And the ghost of Grung had said that he had hidden the ball where it would be in plain sight some of the time. Suddenly Cap remembered something about Grung and swimming. Grung could have fastened it under the drawbridge when he went for a swim. When the drawbridge was up, people across the moat would see the ball plainly.

Cap thought of his own fortune: *Keep an eye on ups and downs.* A drawbridge went up and down.

Cap saw Lisa cowering as Sprod raised his spell sprinkler. "Stop!" he shouted. "I've got it! I know where the crystal ball is!"

11

The Crystal Ball

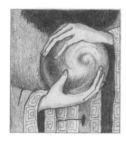 Sprod stared at Cap suspiciously, but he lowered his spell sprinkler. "If this is some sort of trick," he said, "I warn you: There will be no flies for you later."

"It's no trick," Cap said firmly. Then he whispered to Lisa. "Remember what you thought was a brown eye on the bottom side of the drawbridge? It was brown because wood showed through it."

She clapped her hands and gave Cap a huge hug.

"Everybody come with me above the drawbridge," Cap said. "Sir Baggish, bring a rope, will you? I'll need your help to recover the ball."

Baggish brought a velvet-covered rope that had once been used to keep sweaty peasants from venturing too far into the room. The duke led the way across the courtyard and up some steps to a parapet above the gate and drawbridge.

Cap looked down the face of the drawbridge and saw something round and shining. "Do you see that bulge?" he said to Sir Baggish. "Tie a loop that I can sit in, and lower me down there."

Baggish made a seat out of one end of the rope, and Cap slipped in and hung on. As he was lowered closer and closer to the round object, he held his breath. If he was wrong about it, no hope remained.

Suddenly Cap was at eye level with the object. He was almost afraid to touch it, but he reached out and ran a finger over its fine smooth surface. Excitement filled him. He could see that a shallow hole as wide as two fists had been gouged out of a plank, and the sphere had been cemented in there. It couldn't be anything but the crystal ball!

Placing his hand against it, Cap dug carefully with his pocketknife. The ball came loose, and he clutched it tightly for fear of dropping it. It seemed clearer than ordinary glass.

"I have it!" he shouted to the people watching from above. He held the crystal ball high so that it gleamed in the sun. "Lift me back, Sir Baggish."

At that instant Cap felt something cold and clammy surround his hands. A force was pulling the crystal ball away from him.

"No!" Cap shouted, determined not to lose it at the last minute. Swaying on the rope, he jerked back and forth until he broke the freezing grip. He clamped the ball against his chest with both hands.

Icy fingers grasped his wrists. Although the sun shone too brightly for him to see the ghost, Cap knew that it was Grung. Cold crept into his fingers, and he feared that he would lose his hold after all.

"Hurry!" he called desperately to Baggish. "Pull me up as fast as you can! Grung is trying to seize the ball! He probably wants to steal it and hide it again!"

As fast as he could, Baggish hauled Cap to the parapet and lifted him over the side onto its platform. Cap rolled onto his hands and knees, hoping to bury the ball beneath him. He felt Grung's arms around him, trying to wrest the ball away.

No one on the parapet was carrying a

torch. "Sprod!" Cap called out. "If you want your crystal ball, get rid of Grung!"

The wizard shook his spell sprinkler. A few drops fell toward Cap.

Oh, no, Cap thought, not a toad! But nothing happened, except that in a few seconds he felt his wrists released and his fingers grow warmer. Looking up, he saw a ghostly toad, its head in the right place, hopping away into the shadows of the parapet.

With Baggish's help, Cap got up, pressing the crystal ball safely against his chest. He smiled at everyone. Lisa's face beamed with joy.

"Very good. I'll take my crystal ball now, thank you," Sprod said, holding out his hand.

"Not yet," Cap replied, keeping both his hands around the ball. There were matters to be settled with Sprod first. "Let's go back into the castle."

Sprod muttered under his breath, but he turned around, and everyone followed him down to the grand reception hall. The ghostly toad hopped after them, croaking angrily.

Lisa touched Cap's arm as they entered the hall. "Can I look into it?" she asked.

"Sure," he said, handing the ball to her.

"Be careful," the duke warned her. "Don't ask anything unless you're sure you want to know the answer, and don't waste a question on something you'll figure out in plenty of time anyway. How's that! Two of my wise sayings at once!"

Cupping the ball in both hands, Lisa asked, "How can I make cookies with magic fortunes?"

The crystal ball remained clear.

"Obviously, you can't," Sprod said. "Try something else."

"All right. Where can I get a spell sprinkler?"

Again the crystal ball showed nothing.

"I have the only spell sprinkler in existence, and I won't give it to you," Sprod declared.

Having seen magic work, Lisa was disappointed that she couldn't work some herself. If she told her friends at home about her adventure in the castle, they would probably think she had made it up. She guessed she would have to be content with showing them the butterflies she had caught. That was something, for her collection had grown larger, with beautiful butterflies, over the summer. She wished she could have the best collection anywhere.

"Where can I catch the biggest butterfly in the world?" she asked.

A group of islands, seen from high up, appeared in the crystal ball. As the view narrowed, one island came into focus, then part of the island, and finally a jungle so thick that it made the forest of Beringia seem a meadow.

"But there weren't any names on the islands!" Lisa complained. "How will I find out where they are?"

Bounce was eager to take a turn. "Show me doing what I want to do more than anything," he said, holding the ball and peering into it intently. A smoky cloud appeared, swirled, then vanished. The vision that replaced it showed Bounce juggling two eggs, two plates, a knife, a fork, a spoon, and a tambourine all at the same time—while balancing a ball on one foot and a vase on his head.

"Hooray!" Bounce shouted, tossing the crystal ball in the air joyfully.

As he tried to catch it, it slipped from his hand. Desperately Bounce threw himself to the stone floor, with his legs straight out, and the ball landed softly on his lap.

"I guess juggling will take more practice," Bounce muttered.

Cap glared at Bounce but didn't scold him. He took the ball and thought of asking it where he could have another adventure. But then he decided he would rather know more about this one. "How long ago was this castle enchanted?" he asked.

A blackboard appeared inside the crystal ball. A piece of chalk in an invisible hand wrote the number of the present year, then subtracted the number of the year of enchantment. The difference was seven hundred years.

"I never knew a spell would last so long," Sprod said. "After seven hundred years, I'm surprised it hasn't frayed at the edges and developed thin spots and let the magic seep out. But enough!" he added impatiently. "If you've had your fun, I'll take my ball, and you can take your rewards and go home."

An iron fist clanged on an iron breastplate. The deep voice of Baggish said, "Ahem! While you were busy, I finished the first four lines of my new sonnet for Lady Thistle."

"I'll bet you're going to let us hear it," Thistle remarked.

"If you really want to," Baggish replied. He didn't wait to learn if anybody really wanted to. He boomed out:

My Thistle's eyes are round as a wagon wheel;
Their light makes bright the darkest hour of
    night.
Ne'er spare your sculptured nostrils from my
    sight
Nor shield your lips from learning how I feel.

"Remarkable!" Thistle groaned.

"The second line is especially good, don't
you think?" Baggish asked.

Thistle laughed. "The third line is more
original."

Sprod raised his spell sprinkler as if he
were going to use it to improve the sonnet. Instead, he roared at Cap, "My crystal ball! Give
me my crystal ball! Now!"

Cap held the ball away. "We found it, so
we've earned our freedom, but we never
promised to give it back to you. You have to
earn it. First you have to turn all the toads
back to boys and girls and return them to their
homes."

"Give up my toads!" Sprod muttered to
himself and wiggled his eyebrows. "Oh, very
well." He pointed his spell sprinkler in the direction of his tower rooms, waved it, and then
pointed it at the floor. Suddenly more than a
dozen toads sat blinking near his feet. He drew

an imaginary circle around them with the spell sprinkler and chanted strange words. The toads disappeared.

"Done," Sprod said. "I cast a wagon spell. The magic wagon will drop them off at whatever time and place they came from. Their parents won't even have missed them."

"And now Grung," Cap said.

"Grung? What about Grung?"

"Make him a knight again, and not a ghost."

"You've gone soft in the head. Who wants Grung around?"

"I do, if he behaves himself," Duke Lothrio said. "You can make him promise not to pull any more sneaky tricks."

"Grung!" Sprod shouted. He pointed his spell sprinkler at the floor, and the ghost of a toad hopped into place. "Do you promise not to bother people?" Sprod asked.

The toad ghost tried to hop away, but it appeared to be stuck fast in place. It shook its head no.

"Come now, Sir Grung," Duke Lothrio said. "Be willing to try some honest bashing for a change."

Finally the ghost toad croaked what might have been yes and nodded its head. Sprod touched it with the spell sprinkler, and it turned into a knight in armor.

"You look better with your head in the right place, Sir Grung," Lisa said.

"I was getting used to it under my arm," Grung answered. He shook his head vigorously but couldn't shake it off his neck. Raising his gauntleted hands to stare at them, he said, "I miss my icy grip already. Who wants to be a goody-goody?"

"Anything else?" Sprod asked Cap.

"Yes. You have to promise to bring all the people in the castle back to life, and you have to promise never to force anyone to do anything for you unless he agrees first."

"He or she," Lisa said.

"He or she," Cap repeated.

"They've got you, Sprod," the duke said with a laugh. "I never thought I'd see anybody get the best of our famous wizard."

Cap waited while Sprod shuffled his feet and mumbled to himself. Finally Sprod said, "I promise."

"One more thing, if you don't mind," said the duke. "Remove the spell of invisibility from the castle, Sprod, and let down the drawbridge."

Sprod waved his spell sprinkler around and

around before he said, "There. It's hard to do a spell backwards. And now I have to cast another spell to take the castle and its people back where we belong. That's when the people will revive."

"You can do that as soon as Cap and Lisa leave."

Cap gave Sprod the crystal ball. The wizard turned without a word and walked away.

"Now it's time for rewards," the duke announced. He went to a chest, which was guarded by two men who were at the moment too paralyzed to stop a robber on crutches, and took leather pouches from it. "Diamonds, rubies, emeralds, pearls, sapphires," he said, spilling them out. "Take what you want."

Cap and Lisa looked at the jewels in amazement.

"Thanks," Cap said, "but people would think we stole them. They'd never believe we had been to an invisible castle. All I want is something to prove to myself that I was here. How about one of the banners hanging on the wall?"

"You can have my own banner," the duke said. "It has a chessboard painted on it in red and black. Bounce, climb into the rafters and bring it down, will you? Do try not to fall."

"What I would like is one of Lady Thistle's bird tapestries," Lisa said.

"I'll give it to you gladly if you promise to hang it where people who admire birds will see how good it is," Thistle said. She took a small tapestry off the wall for Lisa.

Lisa took her butterfly net from the woman it was leaning against and said, "I guess it's time to go." She hugged Bounce. "I'll miss you. You were fun."

Cap clapped Bounce on the shoulder. "We never would have found the crystal ball if you hadn't bumped your head," he said. "I hope it's not too sore. I'll miss you too."

"I wish you could find the castle again so we could have some fun without a lot of problems," Bounce said. He turned away and wiped a tear from his cheek.

"You young people would be welcome here any time," the duke said.

"Thanks," Cap said. We'll never find the castle after Sprod takes it back seven hundred years, he thought sadly. "And thank you for your banner."

"Thank you for the tapestry," Lisa said to Lady Thistle. "It's beautiful."

Lisa joined Cap in saying good-bye to Bounce and Duke Lothrio and Lady Thistle

and Sir Baggish and even Sir Grung. Everyone came into the courtyard and waved as they crossed the drawbridge. They continued, without encountering the invisible barrier, down into the narrow valley and up into the forest.

When they reached the height from which they had first seen the castle, they heard a loud noise.

"UURRP!" It sounded like a good-bye burp from Sprod.

Turning back, they saw a castle in ruins. Both towers had fallen down. A few crumbling walls still stood, covered with lichens and creepers. The drawbridge had rotted away. Cap and Lisa knew that the moat would be dry.

"Look what happened to the castle," Lisa whispered with awe.

"It's the same thing that happens to most castles, I guess," Cap answered unhappily. "I hope it lasted a long time after Sprod took it back."

"Cap!" Lisa exclaimed. "My tapestry's gone! I had it in my hands. Your banner's gone too!"

Cap looked startled. "You're right. I'm sure I didn't drop it. Maybe it was snatched away without my knowing it." He looked across the valley toward the ruins. "Maybe the tapestry and banner were under the same spell as the rest of the castle and were carried back with it."

"That's no fair. They were our rewards."

"I guess you can't trust magic. Cheer up, Lisa. We got out safely, and we had an exciting adventure and met some neat people we'll never forget."

"I guess so. Especially Bounce."

They found the notches Cap had cut in the trees and followed them back to their cottage.

"You were gone so long I was afraid you were lost," their mother said. "Did you catch any butterflies?"

"No, but we found an old castle," Cap said. "We can show you the ruins."

"Are you hungry? How about a snack?"

Lisa smiled at Cap. "No thanks. A man at the castle gave us some fortune cookies."